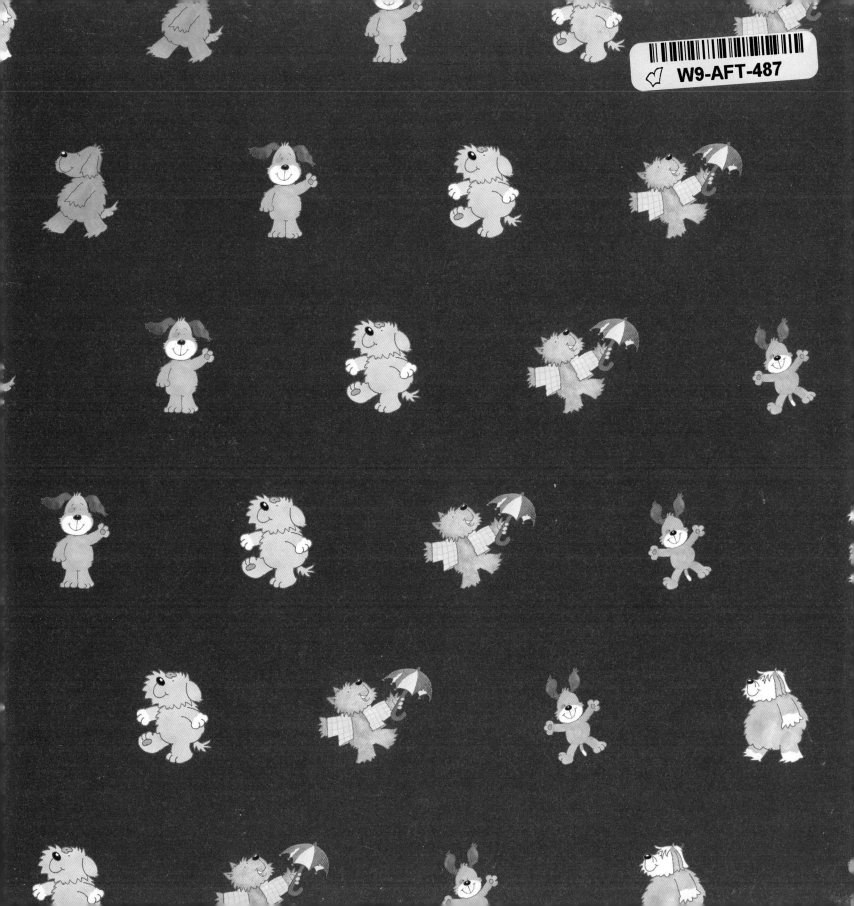

THIS BOOK BELONGS TO...

....

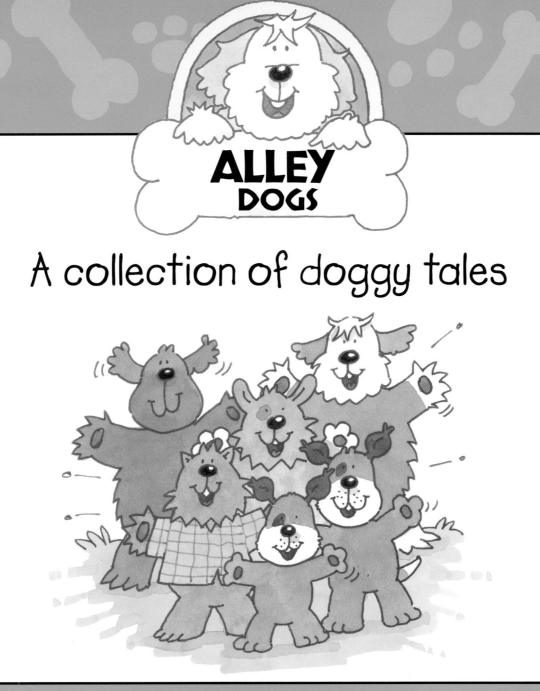

ALLEY DOGS

A collection of doggy tales

Written by Lesley Rees
Illustrated by Terry Burton

This is a Parragon Book
This edition published in 2001
PARRAGON, Queen Street House, 4 Queen Street, Bath
BA1 1HE, UK

Copyright © PARRAGON 2000

Created and produced by THE COMPLETE WORKS

Printed in China

ISBN 0-75256-637-7

Contents

It was the middle of the night.
Harvey and his gang were fast asleep in the
higgledy-piggledy, messy alley, dreaming of
yummy bones and chasing dustmen! The only
sounds were the gentle rumblings of Ruffle's
tummy and Bonnie's snores!

Everyone and everything was fast asleep —
or were they?

Six naughty alley cats peeped over the fence. They spied the snoozing dogs and, grinning and sniggering, they scribbled and scrabbled up the fence.

"I've got an idea!" whispered Archie. "Listen..."

Wibbling and wobbling, the alley cats stood in a line along the top of the fence...

"Those dippy dogs are in for a fright!" giggled Archie.

"I bet I'll be the loudest!" boasted Lenny.

The cats took a deep breath, and out came the scariest, screechiest sounds you ever did hear!

The terrible noise woke Harvey with a start and made him fall off his mattress, straight on to Mac!

"What's that noise?" yelped Mac. "Is it the bagpipe ghost?"

"G-Ghost?" cried Puddles, rushing up to Harvey. "Help!"

The noise made Patchy and Ruffles jump. They fell in a big heap on top of Ruffles' bed! "Save us!" they cried.

Harvey spotted the culprits. "Oh, it's just those pesky pussies," he groaned, "up to mischief as usual. Don't worry, everyone, let's just ignore them and go back to sleep."

But those naughty cats weren't finished yet!

"Look!" cried Lenny. "One of them is still asleep. We must try harder."

They were right — Bonnie was still snoring in her dustbin!

"Louder! Louder!" screeched Archie to the others. But could they wake Bonnie? Oh no! She just kept on snoring and snoring and snoring!

"Someone should teach those cats a lesson," growled Mac. "When I was a pup I'd..."

"*Not now, Mac*," shouted the others.

Harvey smiled. He had an idea. The gang huddled together and listened.

"And me! And me!" cried Puddles, squeezing herself in.

21

The cats thought they were so clever. They laughed and wailed even louder!

Then suddenly, Lenny slipped and grabbed Lulu, who grabbed Hattie, who grabbed Bertie, who grabbed Lucy, who grabbed Archie — and they all tumbled headfirst into the pile of boxes and bins!

"Bravo!" woofed the dogs. "More! More!"

The cats squealed and wailed and ran away.
They'd had enough of playing tricks for one day!

"Now to get our own back," chuckled Harvey.

The gang sneaked along the alley as quiet as little mice.

"Ready?" whispered Harvey. "Steady – GO!"

"WOOF! WOOF!"

The ground shook and the cats jumped high into the air.

"Ha-ha!" roared the dogs. "Scaredy cats! Scaredy cats! We've got our own back!"

"I think that's enough frights for one night!" said Harvey.

"You're right," agreed Archie, sheepishly. "Let's all go back to bed. No more tricks tonight."

Just then Bonnie woke up. "Is it '*time-to-get-up*' time?" she asked, rubbing her eyes.

"No!" said Patchy, "it's '*time-for-bed*' time!" and they all laughed and laughed.

"Oh, goody!" yawned Bonnie. "Bedtime! The best time of the day!"

"Oh, Bonnie," smiled Harvey. "What a sleepyhead you are!"

But Bonnie didn't care. With another enormous yawn and a stretch, she turned away and wandered back to her dustbin—she was *soooo* tired!

At last the cats and dogs of the higgledy-piggledy, messy alley snuggled down to sleep, dreaming of yummy bones and chasing dustbin men — and bowls of scrummy fish! The only sounds were the rumblings of Ruffles' tummy and Bonnie's snores.

Everyone and everything was fast asleep — or were they?

"TOOWHIT —
TOOWHOO!"

34

Troublesome Sister

In the higgledy-piggledy, messy alley it was *tidy up time*! Harvey and the gang had worked hard all morning, scribbling and scrabbling in the heaps of junk trying to clean up their home.

At last, the skip was full of rubbish and they could have a break.

All the gang settled down for a snooze, except for Puddles, Harvey's little sister.

"Where's my teddy?" she wondered. "And where's my ish?" Puddles' 'ish' was a blanket she'd had since she was a baby.

It was full of holes and rather smelly, but she loved it lots.

She looked round the alley. "Teddy! Ish!" she called. "Where are you?" She didn't see them peeping out from the top of the skip.

Puddles was always getting into lots of mischief and today she scampered off down the alley, sure that she would find her teddy and ish down there somewhere. Spotting a hole in the fence, she peeped through and saw an old box of toys. "Are teddy and ish in there?" she wondered.

She squeezed and squashed herself through the gap and crept up to the toybox.

"Teddy! Ish! Are you in there?" she called. But they weren't. She did find an old toy mouse, hidden away at the back. "Doesn't anyone love you?" she asked. "You're very soft and cuddly – I'll love you!"

"Come on, Mousey," she giggled. "You come home with me." Puddles was feeling much happier.

But Lulu the kitten wasn't. The mouse was her favourite toy and as Puddles trotted off she began to wail.

"Mummy! Mummy! Come quickly!" she cried.

Hattie, Lulu's mum, appeared through a gap in the fence. "What a terrible noise you're making," she purred. "What is the matter?"

Lulu sobbed and sniffed. "Puddles has taken my Mousey!" cried the kitten.

47

"There, there," purred Hattie, trying to stop the sobs. "Don't you worry, Lulu, we'll soon get Mousey back."

But Lulu just screamed even louder.

Puddles didn't hear poor Lulu crying. She was dancing around the garden with her new friend. "We are having fun, aren't we, Mousey!" she laughed as she skipped along. "Now all I need is an ish."

As she skipped through the garden next door, Puddles saw a tatty, old scarf hanging down from the branch of an apple tree. "Oh look, Mousey!" she cried. "A cuddly ish with no one to love it."

"Well, it's not really an ish," she thought, "but it is very, very soft." She reached up and took one end in her mouth. With a pull and a tug, the scarf floated down. Puddles picked it up and cuddled it. Now she was really happy. She didn't see Lenny, Lulu's brother, fast asleep in the flowerbed.

Lenny woke up with a start and suddenly saw Puddles skipping off along the garden with his favourite scarf— the one he had hung in the tree to use as a swing! He couldn't believe his eyes and began to cry. "Mummy! Mummy!" he wailed.

Hattie and Lulu squeezed through the hedge.

"That naughty Puddles has stolen my scarf," sobbed Lenny.

Hattie sighed. Oh dear, now both her twins were crying.
Something would have to be done about that pup!

Puddles popped through the hedge and ran straight into— the angry alley cats.

"Oh no!" gulped Puddles. "Someone's in trouble, and I think it's *me*!"

Lulu and Lenny were hiding behind Hattie who looked very cross. Puddles was suddenly scared and she began to cry. "H-H-Harvey!" she croaked. "Help me!"

Puddles' wailing woke up Harvey and the gang.

"Is that Puddles I can hear?" said Ruffles. "Yes! Run, Harvey, *run*! Puddles needs your help!"

"Hang on, Puddles," woofed Harvey. "I'm coming!"

And off he ran, as fast as he could go…

56

Harvey burst through the hedge.
"Okay, guys!" he gasped.
"What's all the fuss about?"

The angry alley cats began shouting all at once.

Puddles hid behind her big brother and shivered and shook. Whatever had she done?

There was so much noise that Harvey couldn't hear what anyone was saying.

"QUIET!" he barked. And they were—even the kittens!

"Thank you," said Harvey. "Now then, Hattie, what is all the noise about?"

"That scally wag sister of yours has stolen my twins' favourite toys," grumbled Hattie.

"Did you, Puddles?" asked Harvey, sternly.

"I didn't mean to, Harvey," she cried. "I thought that no one wanted them."

She gave back little Mousey and the tattered and torn scarf. "Sorry, Lulu," she whimpered. "Sorry, Lenny. I only wanted to love them."

"That's okay, Puddles," smiled the twins. "But you see, we love them—lots and lots."

Hattie looked at Puddles and shook her head, she really was an annoying puppy. Harvey gave a huge sigh—panic over!

"Puddles, you're such a scamp," smiled Harvey.

"But I was only looking for my teddy and my ish," cried Puddles. "I don't know where they are."

"Oh, is that what this is all about?" said Harvey.

He scooped them from the skip and gave them back to Puddles with a hug and a kiss. "Now, no more trouble today," he said. "Let's all have a dog-nap. Okay?"

Puddles hugged her teddy and stroked her ish; she was happy again. "Well," said Puddles, looking at Harvey with a naughty grin, "ish and I will be good, but teddy might not!"

Big Top

It was a grey day in the higgledy-piggledy, messy alley. Harvey and his gang were fed up!

"I'm bored!" moaned Ruffles. "There's nothing to do!"

"What about a game of hide and seek?" asked Harvey.

"Boring! Boring! Boring!" called Puddles, hanging upside down on the fence.

"What we need is some fun!" yawned Bonnie, "I've got an idea…"

Soon Bonnie and Puddles were jumping on an old mattress. BOINGG! BOINGG! BOINGG! They bounced up and down, up and down.

"*This* is fun!" shrieked Puddles. "I bet I can bounce the highest."

"I'm the *Amazing Bouncing Bonnie*," giggled Bonnie. "Look!"

She bounced high into the air — and landed with a thud on a clump of grass! "Ooops a daisy," she said. "I think I missed!"

Then Mac clambered onto the washing line.

"WHEEEE! Look at me! I'm the wibbly wobbly dog."

"Oh no!" gasped Patchy. "Here comes tumble time," as Mac toppled over onto the mattress below. Mac sat up and rubbed his head, grinning.

Harvey laughed. His friends' tricks had given him an idea. "Let's put on a circus," he said.

The alley dogs all agreed and they scampered off to the playground in search of their big top!

"Okay, everyone," said Harvey, when they arrived. "We need to make a circus ring."

"Do you think these old tyres will make good seats?" asked Ruffles.

"They sure will," said Patchy. "And these old plastic bags can be the curtains!"

In no time at all, the big top was ready.

"Well done!" smiled Harvey.

"We must let everyone know that the circus is in town!" said Harvey. "Come on, Ruffles, you've got the loudest voice."

So, Ruffles took a deep breath and boomed out loud, "Roll up! Roll up! Come to Harvey's Big Top. See the Greatest Show on Earth!"

Soon the air was filled with woofing and yapping as their pals queued up to see the circus!

The nervous gang huddled behind the curtain.

"Right," said Harvey. "Who's going first?"

Patchy peeped out. "Not me!" she whispered. "There are far too many dogs out there and I'm a bit shy."

"And I'm still practising!" cried Ruffles.

The others shook their heads; no one wanted to go first. They were all *scaredy cats*!

Harvey took a deep breath and stepped into the ring. "And now, ladies and gentlemen," he cried, "please give a big, warm woof for *Harvey's Amazing Daring Dogs*!"

The audience clapped and stamped their paws! But the gang did not appear.

"Harvey," Mac called, "we've got the doggy-wobbles!"

Harvey crept behind the curtain. His friends were quivering and quaking. "Silly Billies," he smiled. "There's nothing to be scared of. Watch me."

He quickly pulled on a cape and ran back into the ring.

"Let the show begin with *Harvey the Brave*!" he cried, and the audience gave a loud cheer.

"For my first trick," he announced, "the *Tricky Tightrope*!"

He wibbled and wobbled across the top of the swing from one end to the other — and didn't fall off once.

"How does he do it?" gasped the audience, holding their breath in wonder. "Whatever next?"

Harvey climbed to the top of a huge pile of bricks.

"Eeek! What if he falls?" squeaked a little dog. "I can't bear to look."

But Harvey made it — *and* balanced on one paw!

The alley dogs peeped out from behind the curtain. Harvey was having such a good time that it didn't look in the least bit scary. So at last, *Harvey's Amazing Daring Dogs* rushed to join in the fun.

"Look at me," said Ruffles. "I can balance a ball on my tummy."

The audience laughed and cheered and clapped.

Patchy and Mac tumbled and turned on their bouncy mattress—what a pair of acrobats!

The show ended with the dangerous and daring *Trolley Trick*. Everyone held their breath. Bonnie and Ruffles stood on the bottom, Patchy and Mac climbed onto their shoulders and little Puddles balanced on the very tip top. When they were ready, Harvey pushed the trolley round and round the ring.

"More! More!" roared the crowd, as the show came to an end.

"Well, Puddles," smiled Harvey, when they finally got back to their higgledy-piggledy, messy alley, "was that boring, boring, boring?"

"Oh no, Harvey," she said. "It wasn't boring, it was **fun, fun, fun!**"

The
End

In the higgledy-piggledy, messy alley it was a *very* hot day. Harvey and his gang were melting!

"I need a slurpy, slippy ice lolly," sighed Ruffles.

"I need a cool pool to roll in," squeaked Puddles.

Those hot dogs just didn't know what to do!

"It's even too hot to sleep," complained Bonnie. "I'm the hottest dog in the whole world!"

"I bet I'm hotter than you!" snorted Ruffles.

"Oh no, you're not," replied Patchy. "I am!"

"I haven't been this hot," said Mac, "since I was in the desert when…"

"*Not now, Mac*!" the other dogs all yelled together.

"Stop!" cried Harvey. "It's much too hot to argue! Listen, I know what we'll do…"

"Let's play a game. Let's have a—water hunt."

"Can I hunt, too?" yelped Puddles, hopping from one hot paw to the other.

"Do we have to move, Harvey?" groaned Patchy. "I don't think I can."

"Come on," said Harvey. "Where can we find some water?"

"I'm too hot to think," wailed Bonnie.

"We're too hot to do *anything*," said Patchy.

"Except nosh yummy ice cold ice cream," replied Ruffles, with a grin.

"I know," cried Mac suddenly. "Let's go to the seaside! We could play in the sand and splish and splash in the water."

"Good thinking, Mac," smiled Harvey. "But it's too far for us to go on a day like today. Can you think of something else?"

"I've got a *really* good idea," said Ruffles.

"What is it?" asked Bonnie.

"Diggin'!" grinned Ruffles.

"Digging?" cried the others. "Dig for water in this heat?"

"No," said Ruffles excitedly. "Dig for bones. The dirt will be really damp and cool and we could roll around in it and…"

"No way, Ruffles," said Harvey firmly. "Today is *not* a digging day."

"Let's all go to the park," suggested Patchy. "We could jump in and out of the paddling pool and play in the fountain."

Poor Puddles looked as though she were going to burst into tears.

"I can't walk that far, Harvey," she whispered. "I've only got little legs!"

"Don't worry, Puddles," said Harvey kindly. "We wouldn't go without you."

"Oh, there *must* be some water somewhere!" puffed and panted Patchy.

"If I don't find water soon, I'm going to melt into a big, hairy puddle!" groaned Ruffles.

"Haven't you got *any* ideas at all, Harvey?" asked Mac.

But even Harvey was too hot to think, and Bonnie had given up and had gone to sleep in her dustbin!

Those poor hot dogs — what on earth could they do?

Meanwhile, the sizzling alley cats were searching, too. But they weren't on a water hunt. Oh no! They were on a mouse hunt — Archie had lost his favourite toy mouse!

"I WANT IT BACK!" wailed Archie, looking under a box.

"Well, it's not in here!" called Bertie from the top of a flower pot.

"Phew!" groaned Hattie. "It's way too hot for hunting, Archie. Why don't we have a cat nap instead?"

"Cat nap time!" said Lucy. "Great idea."

So the alley cats snuggled down for an afternoon nap — or did they?

Lenny and Lulu — the two little kittens — weren't quite ready for a nap just yet!

"Naps are for babies," whispered Lenny to his sister. "Come on, Lulu, follow me."

"Yippee!" giggled Lulu. "An adventure."

The kittens clambered and climbed over the pots and pans and headed towards a hole in the fence.

"Hey, Lulu!" cried Lenny. "I bet we find Archie's mouse through here."

So, carefully and quietly, the kittens squeezed themselves through the tiny gap...

Suddenly, a strange, stripey monster jumped out in front of them!

"AAAAAGH!" screamed Lulu. "What is it?"

Swooping and swaying through the spikey grass, the monster wiggled and wiggled towards them. Then it lifted up its head and gave a loud, angry "HISSSSS!"

"It's a snake!" yelled Lenny. "Let's scarper."

Running as fast as they could, the kittens bounded towards a tree trunk and scampered up into its branches!

"We'll be safe up here," gasped Lenny.

But Lenny was wrong!

The sinister snake hissed louder and louder and slithered up the tree after them.

Lenny and Lulu quivered and quaked.

"HELP!" they wailed.

As the snake swayed about in front of the kittens, the poor little pussies began to cry.

With one, last enormous "HISSSSSSS!", the swinging snake leapt towards them — and got stuck in a branch!

Suddenly a great big spurt of water gushed from the snake's mouth, shot over the fence and into the alley below – SPLOOOSH!

Those silly scally wags. It wasn't a snake at all. It was a hosepipe and the cool refreshing water woke up Harvey and the gang – they couldn't believe their eyes!

"It's rainy and sunny at the same time," laughed Harvey.

He looked up and saw Lenny and Lulu peeping shyly over the fence.

"You clever cats," he called up to them.

"Three cheers for Lenny and Lulu!" cried Harvey. "HIP! HIP! HOORAY!"

And so, two cool cats had made five hot dogs very happy!

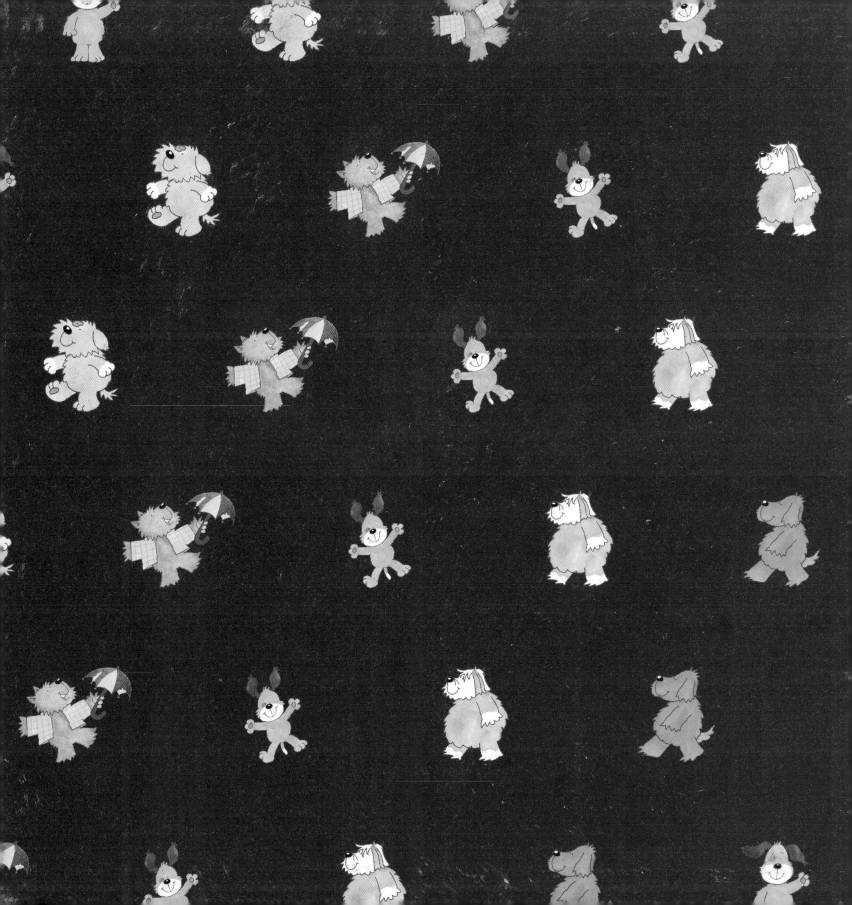